PHONICS CHAPTER BOOK 4

The Case
of the
Missing Monkeys

by Alice Pernick
Illustrated by Chris Demarest

Scholastic Inc.
New York   Toronto   London   Auckland   Sydney

No part of this publication may be reproduced in whole or in part, or stored in a retrieval system, or transmitted in any form or by any means, electronic, mechanical, photocopying, recording, or otherwise, without written permission of the publisher. For information regarding permission, write to Scholastic Inc., Instructional Publishing Group, 555 Broadway, New York, N. Y. 10012.

Copyright © 1998 by Scholastic Inc.
Scholastic Phonics Chapter Books in design is a trademark of Scholastic Inc.
All rights reserved. Published by Scholastic Inc.
Printed in the U.S.A.
ISBN 0-590-03079-5

8 9 10   23   04 03 02 01

Dear Teacher/Family Member,

Scholastic Phonics Chapter Books provide early readers with interesting stories in easy-to-manage chapters. The books in this series are controlled for sounds and common sight words. Once sounds and sight words have been introduced, they are repeated frequently to give children lots of reading practice and to build children's confidence. When children experience success in reading, they want to read more, and when they read more, they become better readers.

Phonics instruction teaches children the way words work and gives them the strategies they need to become fluent, independent readers. However, phonics can only be effective when reading is meaningful and children have the opportunity to read many different kinds of books. Scholastic Phonics Chapter Books cover many curricular areas and genres. They are carefully designed to help build good readers, but more importantly, to inspire children to love reading.

Contents

1 Days at the Zoo

What would happen if wild animals ran away from a zoo? What if the zoo was near where you lived?

Well, that's just what happened one day to the people who live near the San Francisco Zoo. The five Patas (**pat**-uhss) monkeys who lived at the zoo ran away.

Would you want to help find the missing monkeys? Before you looked for the monkeys, you would have to know what Patas monkeys look like. Patas monkeys are the color of rust. They may have some white on their faces, too. They have long tails. Each monkey is about the size of a cat.

A family of Patas monkeys has only one male and many females. This family of Patas monkeys at the San Francisco Zoo had one male monkey and four female monkeys. The monkeys came from a place that is a long way from San Francisco. They came from a place where the days are hot. Now the monkeys have a new home to live and play in.

At the zoo, there is a heated room where the monkeys sometimes stay. They also stay in an outside pen. There is grass and there are swaying trees in the outside pen.

You might think that the monkeys would jump up onto the trees and find a way out. But the pen has very high glass walls which keep the monkeys in. The Patas monkeys seem happy to stay in their home on the ground.

Every day, zoo keepers lay down grapes and bananas in hiding places.

That way the monkeys have to work to find the food. After they eat, the monkeys may spend the day cleaning each other and playing.

All was well until one day, when all five monkeys ran away from their pen. Two of the monkeys stayed away for more than a week.

Where do you think those two monkeys went? How do you think they would get back to the zoo? Which way would you go if you were a monkey on the loose?

2 One Rainy Night

How did the monkeys get out of their pen? Did they make up a plan? Did they use vines to make a swing and sail over the glass wall? Did they crawl through a water drain-pipe? Did they wait and hop on a passing train? Now, most monkeys are very smart, but their brains couldn't think up plans like that.

What really happened was this. One very rainy night there was a strong wind. It made a tree fall down right into the monkeys' pen. The tree lay by the wall and made a bridge from the ground all the way to the top of the pen.

As you may know, most monkeys are very curious. They want to know everything. If they see something new, they can't help but find out all about it.

So that rainy night when the tree fell down, the monkeys jumped onto the tree and followed the trail. Those curious monkeys had to see where this trail might take them. The trail took them up to the top of the glass wall. From there, they went over the wall, jumped down, and then they were free!

The zoo keepers almost fainted when they looked in the monkeys' pen and saw that there were no monkeys! But the zoo keepers were very lucky. The day after the rain, they found all five monkeys sitting just outside of their pen.

A very big crowd of people came. They were happy to see the monkeys, but it was plain to see that Popp, the male monkey, was not happy to see them. There were so many people that Popp could not wait to get back home. He just followed the trail and went right back down the tree and into the pen.

Most of the time, a female Patas monkey will follow after a male Patas monkey. That day, two of the female monkeys followed Popp down the trail back to the pen.

The other two female monkeys, White Eyes and Mole, did not follow. They did not stop to wait for anything, but just ran away.

Where were those two curious monkeys aiming to go?

The zoo keepers saw one of the monkeys. But then the monkey jumped over the main rail that went around the zoo. She was last seen running to the big lake on the other side of the street.

No one knew where the last monkey went. It was plain to see that the zoo keepers couldn't wait and needed to do something fast. Now there were two monkeys missing.

Where were those curious monkeys?

3 Those Hard-to-Find Monkeys

Finding those two smart monkeys was going to be hard. Patas monkeys move very quickly and climb very well, so it's hard to chase them.

If the zoo keepers could not chase the monkeys, what were they going to do? How were the monkeys going to live in the cold and rain of San Francisco, far away from their heated home at the zoo? How would they find food to eat outside of the zoo park?

The zoo keepers hoped that the monkeys would be smart and come home to the zoo park. Maybe they would climb back down the tree on their own. Maybe the sounds of the other animals in the zoo park might help the monkeys find their way home through the dark night.

The zoo keepers went on TV and asked people to call the zoo if they saw the monkeys. After that, many people called. Most calls were silly and didn't help. Some people called and started making monkey sounds. Others called to say that the monkeys were in gardens and parks very far from the zoo.

The zoo keepers got one curious call
from a woman. The woman told them
that she saw one monkey in her yard.
When the woman let her cat out, the
monkey darted away.

Then a man called to say he saw a monkey in his yard. The zoo keepers came to his house. They saw the monkey, too, but the monkey quickly darted away.

The zoo keepers had another smart plan. They went out looking for the monkeys. People all over San Francisco helped them. Some people used special glasses. They looked through the glasses to spot the monkeys, but they didn't find them.

The zoo keepers also started to put out food in places around the park where people said they had seen the monkeys. Then the zoo keepers would look for footprints where they had left the food. From the marks left in the mud, a zoo keeper could tell which animal had made them.

Looking at the left-over food was another smart thing that the zoo keepers did. They wanted to see if they could tell which kind of animal had been there. One day they found a banana peel in one part of the zoo park.

The zoo keepers said that the banana was eaten by one of the missing Patas monkeys. They said that another kind of animal would have eaten the banana and the peel, too. Another kind of animal would have eaten only part of the banana and left teeth marks. But a monkey was special. It would know how to peel a banana, just eat what was inside, and leave the peel.

The last thing the zoo keepers did was to try to trap the monkeys. Trapping monkeys is hard because monkeys are very smart. If the trap doesn't work the first time, the monkey will never go near another trap.

How would you outsmart a monkey? The trick is to start by putting a banana near the outside of the trap. If the monkey eats that one, you put another banana inside the trap. With any luck, the monkey will go through the trap to get that banana. Then you shut the trap quickly.

Now the zoo keepers just had to wait for something to happen. That was the hard part!

4 No More Missing Monkeys

The zoo keepers waited, day after day, for their monkeys to come home. For more than a week after the storm, the zoo keepers still could not get the two monkeys to come back.

Then, one morning, they found White Eyes sitting in a trap. The banana trick had worked! They opened the trap and gave her water to drink. White Eyes was in good shape.

Now just Mole was missing.

Soon there was good news. Mole was spotted on the street that runs from the shore to the zoo. The man who saw her said that at first she looked like a cat. Then he saw that she was the missing monkey.

The zoo keepers came to see. They followed Mole for a short time until they saw her come back into the zoo. The next morning, she was spotted not far from the pen where the apes lived.

That same day, more people spotted Mole in places around the zoo. The zoo keepers were sort of lucky. They didn't have to do anything more to get Mole back. All they had to do was wait.

Soon Mole was ready to come home. She climbed onto a ledge, up to the top of the glass wall, and then jumped back into her pen.

You know that monkeys are very curious. So what do you think a curious monkey does when another monkey comes home after a short trip? Does it pat the monkey on the back? Does it hug the monkey?

The zoo keepers opened a door and put White Eyes and Mole in a room with a glass wall. They put the other three monkeys in the room next door. For a while, the monkeys just looked at each other through the glass.

Then the zoo keepers put the monkeys together. The three monkeys looked at White Eyes and Mole in a funny way. The zoo keepers said it seemed as if they were saying, "Where were you? What did you do? Tell us your story."

What does a zoo do for its lost monkeys when they come home? The zoo keepers were so happy to see all of the monkeys together that they went to a food store and made a big party for them. There were sweets for the people. There were grapes and seeds for the monkeys. Those five monkeys ate more and more as the day went on.

After the party, the zoo keepers made footprints of each monkey's feet. The footprints would help them if a monkey ran away again. Then the zoo keepers could look for footprints in the mud that looked like the footprints of the missing monkey.

Soon life was the same as before for the monkeys. They still came out to look for the grapes and bananas that the zoo keepers put in their pen. They still liked to spend time cleaning each other and playing.

At the zoo, more and more people came to see the monkeys. They all talked about the story of the missing Patas monkeys.

Most of all they wanted to know what happened to White Eyes and Mole in the short time they were away from the zoo. What was the real story? Where did they go? Whom did they meet?

No one but White Eyes and Mole will ever know the real story.

Decodable Words With the Phonic Elements

1 ay

away	play
day	stay
lay	swaying
may	way

2 ai

aiming	rain
brains	rainy
drain	sail
fainted	trail
main	train
plain	wait
rail	

3 ar

dark	outsmart
darted	park
far	part
gardens	smart
hard	start
marks	yard

4 or

before	short
for	sort
more	store
morning	storm
shore	story